PIG the WINNER

FIRST

AWARD
for
THIRD PLACE

Trevor

For the girl who cried silver tears.

First published in Australia in 2016 by Scholastic Press, an imprint of Scholastic Australia Pty Ltd.

ISBN 978-1-338-26845-4

12 11 10 9 8 7 6 5 4 3 2 1   18 19 20 21 22 23

Printed in the U.S.A.   76

This edition first printing, January 2018

The artwork in this book is acrylic (with pens and pencils) on watercolor paper.
The type was set in Adobe Caslon.

PIG the WINNER

the PUG

Aaron Blabey

SCHOLASTIC INC.

Pig was a pug
and I'm sorry to say,
if he didn't come first,
it would ruin his day.

Yes, Pig was a winner.
He just had to win.
And nothing would stop him.
Oh, where to begin?

Believe it or not,
he was quite hard to beat.

And the reason was simple . . .

yes, Pig was a cheat.

But if he did lose,
he'd throw a pink fit.
He'd scream and he'd cry
and he just wouldn't quit.

He'd sob and he'd sulk
with a quivering chin,
till you gave up and said to him,
"OK. You win."

But as soon as you said it,
he'd clap and he'd stamp,
and he'd rub it in loudly
that he was the champ.

Trevor would say to him,
"Let's just have fun."
But Pig would reply —

"It ain't fun
till I've
WON!"

So one night at supper,
Pig shouted with glee,
"Who can eat faster?
I bet that it's me!"

Trevor said shyly,
"I don't want to race."
But Pig had yelled,

"GO!"

and was stuffing his face.

He wolfed down his food.
He gobbled his kibble.
His face was awash
with biscuits and dribble.

He chomped up three sausages—
all of them whoppers!
Then he munched through his doggie treats,
gnashing his choppers.

He swallowed it all in a minute or less.

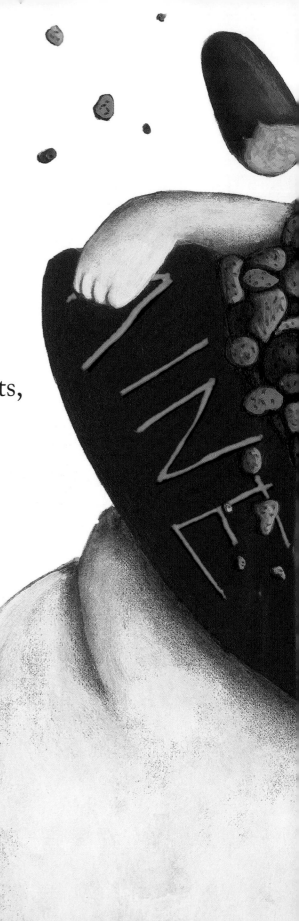

But something went wrong.

Do you know?
Can you guess?

Because he was busy
stuffing his hole,
Pig didn't notice . . .

he'd swallowed his bowl.

Lucky for Pig,
Trevor knew what to do.
He squeezed out the bowl
before Pig could turn blue.

But Pig didn't thank him!
He just said,

"I WIN!"

Then the bowl bounced right back . . .

. . . and knocked Pig in the bin.

These days it's different,
I'm happy to say.
Pig's not the winner
each time that they play.

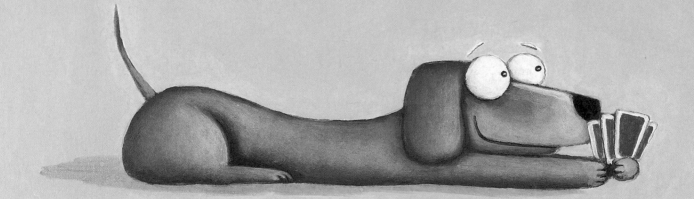

He plays to have fun,
and his tantrums have ceased.
Yes, Trevor can win now!

Well, sometimes, at least.